This Is About
The Body,
The Mind,
The Soul,
The World,
Time, and Fate

STORIES BY

DIANE WILLIAMS

This Is About The Body, The Mind, The Soul, The World, Time, and Fate

Grove Weidenfeld

New York

Published by Grove Weidenfeld
A Division of Wheatland Corporation
841 Broadway
New York, New York 10003-4793

Published in Canada by General Publishing Company, Ltd.

Acknowledgment is made to the following publications, in which these stories
appeared:

Agni: "Science and Sin or Love and Understanding"; *Art Dog:* "There Should
Be Nothing Remarkable"; *Conjunctions:* "All American," "The Kind You Know
Forever," "Life After Death," "My Female Honor Is of a Type," "The Nub,"
"Pornography," "Ten Feet from It," "The Uses of Pleasure"; *The Crescent Review:*
"The Waiter"; *Epoch:* "Glass of Fashion"; *The Gettysburg Review:* "OK for Peo-
ple"; *The Ohio Review:* "Marriage and the Family"; *The Quarterly:* "Baby,"
"Boys!," "Dropping the Masters," "Egg," "Forty Thousand Dollars," "The
Hero," "Killer," "Lady," "Mystery of the Universe," "The Nature of the Mira-
cle!," "Oh, My God, the Rapture!," "Passage of the Soul," "Power," "Scream-
ing," "To Die," "Ultimate Object."

Library of Congress Cataloging-in-Publication Data

Williams, Diane.
This is about the body, the mind, the soul, the world, time, and
fate: stories/by Diane Williams.—1st ed.
ISBN 1-55584-368-9   p.   cm.
I. title.
PS3573.I44846T47   1990
813'.54—dc20   89-8949
                                                      CIP

Manufactured in the United States of America
This book is printed on acid-free paper
Designed by Irving Perkins Associates
First Edition
1   3   5   7   9   10   8   6   4   2

CONTENTS

v

vi

vii

This Is About
The Body,
The Mind,
The Soul,
The World,
Time, and Fate

LADY

S he said *please*. Her face looked something more than bitter, with hair which it turned out was a hat, which came down over her ears, which was made of fake fur, which she never removed from her head. She had glasses on. Everything she wore helped me decide to let her in.

She wore flat black patent-leather shoes with pointed toes, with black stockings, wrinkled at the ankles, with silver triangles set in on top of the toes of the shoes to decorate them, and she had on a long black coat, and she was shorter than I am.

Her skin was a bleak sort of skin, and there was no beauty left in her—maybe in her body.

I felt that this lady is fast, because she was at the place where I keep my red rotary-dial phone before I was, after I said, "The phone is in here."

She said, "I know the number."

Sitting on the arm of my sofa, she dialed while her knees were knocking into and tipping back onto two legs my too-small table, which my phone sits on, and my oversized brass lamp, which sits on the table too, with the huge shade, might have crashed. The lamp was clanging, ready to go. She got it back.

She said, "*Merla!*" into the phone receiver.

I knew it—she must have known it—Merla knew it too, that Merla was only a matter of one hundred to two hundred yards from my house, because this woman I had let in, she had told me right off the house number she was looking for. She was telling Merla that it was *impossible* to get to her, that there was no way on earth, that she had kept on running into this east-west street.

"A nice picture," she said to me. She had gotten herself up. She was looking at all of those men dressed for one of the dark-age centuries, marching through foliage, trekking around a hunched-up woman at a well, with their weird insignias on their chests, that nobody I know can figure out, with their faces—version after version of the same face.

She said, "I have a"—something something—"reproduction—" I cannot remember the dates or the royal reign to which she referred, when she was toying with this miniature chair that I have, grabbing it by its arm, and swiveling it on the clubbed foot of one leg, as she was leaving, after everything had been agreed upon with Merla. She would not be getting out of her car for Merla. Merla would meet her at the corner. Merla would.

She, the lady, must have been curious or put off by the jumble of dirty things at my front door that I suppose she first noticed when she was leaving, or by the splendor of my living room just off from the jumble. She missed going inside of it to see what was going on in each of the pictures in there.

What this woman had done to me was incalculable, and she had done it all in a period of time which had lasted no more than five minutes, which so many others have done, coming in here only for the telephone, because I had waved at her while she was shouting at Merla, I had said, "Would it help you to know the number of *this* house?"

Then I had told this little person my wrong address, not because I wanted to, nor because of any need on my part to make up a lie.

I said 2-7-0 which is way off the track, except for two digits, but I had rearranged them, the 7 and the 0, but I did not know I had done that. All that I knew was that I had done something unforgivably uncivil.

It was a lapse to reckon with. I took her into my arms, so that she could never leave me, and then jammed her up into the corner with the jumble by the front door and held her in there, exhausting myself to keep her in there. I didn't care. It hurt her more than it hurt me, to be a lady.

Violence is never the problem. Love at first sight is.

5

THE NATURE
OF THE MIRACLE

The green glass bottle rolled into, rolled out of my arms, out of my hands, and then exploded, just as it should, when it hits our bluestone floor, and spreads itself, and sparkling water, on the territory it was able to cover from our refrigerator to the back door.

The bottle used to fit tightly in my hand, easily, by the neck, and the way one thing leads to another in my mind, this means I should run away from my marriage.

I should run to the man who has told me he does not

want me. He does not even like me. Except for once he took me, and my head was up almost under his arm, my neck was, and my hand went up his back and down his back, and he copied what I did to him on my back with his hand, so that I would know what it would be like, I would have an idea, and then I could run home to my marriage afterward, which is what I did before, after we were done with each other; and the way one thing leads to another in my mind, this means I should run to the man for more of it, but the way one thing leads to another, first I will tell my husband, "I would not choose you for a friend," then I will run to the other man, so that I can hear him say the same thing to me.

This is unrequited love, which is always going around so you can catch it, and get sick with it, and stay home with it, or go out and go about your business getting anyone you have anything to do with sick, even if all that person has done is push the same shopping cart you pushed, so that she can go home, too, and have an accident, such as leaning over to put dishwasher powder into the dishwasher, so that she gets her eye stabbed by the tip of the bread knife, which is drip-drying in the dish rack. It is a tragedy to lose my eye, but this heroism of mine lasted only a matter of moments.

ORGASMS

I swear I did not have anything of hers except for my dark idea of her which I have been keeping to myself until now.

Even better than catching my own husband in the act with her, I opened my mouth, but I left her probably forever, before I made a statement.

She was presiding with her face flattened by some shadow. Her shoulders and her arms, and all across the front of her also were gray which was what made the idea of her dark.

I saw the top half of her blotted out—more than half of what was behind her—nothing more, except some of her black hair curled away up into the—the way hair will, the way hers did. What of it?

If you care, it was like, like going by her like I was this big fish swallowing a big big fish whole, but because I am bigger, and what of it?

She kept on having orgasms with my husband.

The orgasms—where do they go?—crawling up into—as if they could have—up into—dying to get in, ribbed and rosy, I saw seashells were the color mouths should be, or the nipples of breasts, or the color for a seam up inside between legs, or, for I don't care where. Since they are pretty is why I collect them.

KILLER

Past the shimmering gewgaws on the velvet shoes at N-M, I went on by them, chasing two women, especially the one in the raccoon coat, who is glamorous—Marlene—my neighbor's new third wife—he had to have—a divorcee with five children, a convert from Catholicism for him for love—I was on her side. They are all so devout.

I adore I adore I adore—she should have said, I love only you, when she took what I had to give her away from me, because the sunglasses on the counter where I had just paid for my lunch might have been hers, and they *were* hers! She said something ecstatic and I hardly had to do anything, except ride back down the escalator, past pricey purses, veering nearly into jewels, and then into the jewels, where I said no, then on out the huge doors of N-M. I needed to go along over the black pavement, stamping and looking, and, bingo, with my instinct, I would see my car. Postponing the joy of getting into it, for what I would be doing next, I stood and took in the air, and looked around at so much air.

You know how it can hug you and kiss you all over because it is all over you anyway, and inside of me, and I was out there like a smoker—not to try to smother my lungs—just to have something to do with my fingers, and with my hands, and with my mouth, pressing them up against absolutely nothing at all, or aiming to get through it, when there is not a human being I know of who wants to do it with me, my feelings are hurt, when all they would have to do is bat their eyes at me and I would consider myself half the way there.

He doesn't have to stand on his head. Who cares what he does? I think my luck will hold for me. Yesterday they picked up Squeaky Fromme—two men did, after her breakout out of jail. Her being wanted, it didn't go on overly long.

ALL AMERICAN

The woman, who is me—why pretend otherwise?—wants to love a man she cannot have. She thinks that is what she should do. She should love a man like that. He is inappropriate for some reason. He is married.

When she thinks of the man, she thinks *force*, and then whoever has the man already is her enemy—which is the man's wife.

The woman makes sure the man falls in love with her. She has fatal charm. She can force herself to have it. Then she tells the man she cannot love him in return. She says, "You are in the camp with the enemy."

Of course, the woman knew the man was sleeping with the enemy before she ever tried to love him, and the word *enemy* gives joy—the same as I get when the wrong kind of person calls me *darling*, as when my brother says, "Okay," to me, "goodbye, darling," before he hangs up the phone, after we have just made some kind of pact, which is what we should do, because I have to force myself to love the ones I am supposed to love, and then I have to force myself on the ones I am not supposed to love.

I got my first real glimpse of this kind of thing when I was still a girl trying to force myself on my sister. I didn't know what I was doing until it was obvious. We were in the back seat of the family car. The car had just been pulled into the garage. The others got out, but we didn't. I thought I was not done with something. Something was not undone yet—something like that—and I was trying to kiss my sister, and I was trying to hug my sister, and she must have thought it was inappropriate, like what did I think I was a man and she was a woman?

I must have been getting rough, because she was getting hysterical. I remember I was surprised. I remember knowing then that I was applying force and was getting away with it.

THE UNCANNY

Her silver hair ornament was awfully big. I saw a great emerald-diamond ring. I saw the platter of steak tartare leave its position near me and then dive away into the party crowd on the back lawn. Then I saw my own husband having the meat on a Ritz cracker. I saw it in his hand next to his mouth. I drank my iced drink while it was changing color from a deep gold color that had satisfied me deeply to a gold color that certainly did not.

I asked Mrs. Gordon Archibald what she would have

done with all of the people if it had rained. I gave her a suggestion for an answer she could give me which was an antisocial answer. She had a different antisocial answer for me of her own.

After this, my husband and I went off to a dinner club where there was dancing, where a woman touched my earring. She got it to move, saying, "These are buckets!"

My husband said to me while I was swooning in his arms, "Why are all the longest dances the draggiest?"

I took this to mean that he has not loved me for a very long time. Everything means something, or it does not. I have expressed an opinion. Every effect has a source that is not unfamiliar. It's all so evil.

CLAUDETTE'S HEAD

Heddy had no baby. Then we saw Heddy pluck the baby out from somebody's arms. Heddy's face when she turned to us, holding the baby, exposed the feelings any competent woman of this century could have in my opinion. I didn't think it then, but I think it now.

Heddy brought the baby to us.

The baby was curled into her arm and into her breast, and was not crying. It was not at all one of those forlorn babies.

I have seen a face on a baby just after the delivery that made me think you could dress the baby up in a business suit and it could, just as it was, go to the office and run things splendidly. Not this baby. But this baby, which belonged to Heddy's sister, with its good nature, was reassuring to me, which meant absolutely the world at the time.

That's the moment I chose to tell Heddy's sister about the stranger-than-fiction newspaper account I had read the night before, when Heddy gave the baby back to her sister for its bottle.

I said, "Tell me if this surprises you," after I told her what the story was about. Heddy's sister Claudette is an emergency-care doctor, who selected that specialty, she had said, because she likes the variety and the surprise of it.

It probably was not fear I saw in Claudette. It was probably discomfort I saw. The baby probably had been stepping on her arm, pinching her, or scratching her, or something, when I said, "It's about a woman delivering her own baby—one of *those* stories."

Claudette said, "I am trying—" and by then she had the baby in a sitting posture in her lap, and she had the nipple of the bottle stuck into its mouth.

I don't even want to go into the gory details again of the newspaper story I told Claudette, of that woman giving birth in the airplane bathroom. Suffice it to say, the woman accomplished the birth undiscovered. She traveled then, afterward, unremarkably, from Newark to San Francisco, and the baby was lying under the sink for six more hours—but was not dead.

What I did was I pressured Claudette into saying the story surprised her, because I could tell she was not surprised. But I got her to say with a laugh, "*Any—*" and then I interrupted and filled in for her the rest, until she was shaking her head gaily, yes, yes. What I said was, "There never is any follow-up." I said, "These reports of women who squat in the field, who give birth, and then who carry on in the field with their work, these reports, they never mention for how long those women carry on. These women, down through the ages, could have dropped dead within minutes. Who does the follow-up?" I asked, does she, Claudette, do any follow-up at her hospital, after she gives these patients their emergency care, because Claudette had said she had to make a fast good guess about what was wrong with people. Claudette said she had to use common sense. Claudette said, "It is such a small community." She said, "You hear, and if you really care, you call, and you find out." About her baby, she said, "He always does this. He just plays." About me, of course, she didn't say. I didn't say a word about it either, because my husband was there with us also, listening to every word.

I am terrified I will be found out.

There was a downhill sweep of burnt lawn that I could see out the window behind Claudette's head, which led the eye to the grander blue sweep of a lake with sailboats on it and to the sky, which was not too much—all of it—to take in.

THE KIND
YOU KNOW
FOREVER

I had just met them—the brother and the sister who had fucked each other to see what it would be like. And then they said—either he said or she said—that it was like fucking a brother or a sister, so they never did it again.

That they had fucked each other was gossip intended to warn me away from the brother at the party where I watched the sister spread her legs carelessly, so that anyone—for instance, me—could look up her skirt to see darkness when she was sitting on the sofa.

Her husband was next to her—a thick man in a suit which was too small for him or was just under strain. The suit was ripped, I could see, under the arm at the seam. He had his arm up and around his wife, the sister who had fucked her brother.

I wondered if the husband knew, if he knew everything about her or not. I wondered as I watched her legs, her knees bump together, and then spread apart, and I kept my eye on him, while we were sitting around, but I forgot about the husband altogether while we ate. It was a fine meal we had.

And after that meal, the woman who had tried to warn me away from the brother took me aside. We went together from her kitchen to her bathroom. It was her party, and she led me there, and she closed the door. She said, "Look, you be careful." She said, "He's knocked up six girls."

And I said, "What does that mean?"

Then I saw how her long dark hair moved back and forth on either side of her head while she was moving her head, while her eyes were moving around, but not looking at me, while she was figuring me out. She said, "He got them all pregnant."

And I said, "And he didn't care what happened to them?"

"Yes. That's it," she said. "Now you be careful."

She must have known then her party was almost over, because there wasn't much time left after that. She handed out little wrapped gifts in such a hurry at the door, when we were all saying goodbye—it was such a hurry—I didn't get to see where she was getting all of her gifts from. All of a sudden there was just a gift in my hand, as I was going out the door. At the end of a party, I had never gotten a gift before, not since I was a girl, and then we thought we deserved those gifts. So now, something was turned around.

The gift she gave me was a cotton jewel pouch, in a bright shade of pink, made in India, which snapped shut.

I left the party with the sister-fucker. It was logical. We were near to the same age and we were both pretty for our kind, which must have mattered. Let me not forget to add that his sister was pretty, and that her husband was handsome, and that the woman who gave the party was pretty, and that her husband was handsome too.

The sister-fucker and I had both come to the party alone, and it was his idea that we should leave together. First we stopped at a bar, where we both had some drinks. I held onto a matchbook. I turned it by its four corners while he told me everything he was in the mood to tell me about his life, so that I felt I had known him forever.

Then I told him everything I was in the mood to tell him about my life—everything that mattered. I couldn't say now what that was. Then he said, "Write your phone number on the matchbook," which I did.

I asked him, "Should I write my name too?"

And he said, "No, not your name, just your number."

We were at the door in darkness ready to leave the bar when I gave him the matchbook. He gave me a kiss. He pressed hard on my mouth for the kiss and then I was waiting to see what would happen next.

I still see him backing away covered in the shadows. Then he pushed his hands up into his hair. One of his hands was still holding the matchbook so that the whole matchbook went up into it too, sliding under. He was pushing so hard up into his hair with both hands on either side of his head, that he was pulling the skin of his face up and back. He was turning his eyes into slits. He was making his nose go flat. His mouth at the corners was going up.

I didn't know if he was playing around with me, if he was angry, or if he was trying to figure something out. I didn't ask, What does that mean? Now I think it meant he really cared, but it never made a difference. I have fucked him and fucked him and fucked him, and I have felt all that hair on his head in my hands plenty of times.

THE HERO

My aunt was telling me about them coming to get them after I brought back the second helping of fish for me and the vegetables she asked for—the kind that have barely been cooked that look so festive, even with the film of dressing that dulls them down. I didn't want her to have to get up to get her own, not since she's been sick.

My aunt was saying, "They're going to get us. Hurry! Hurry! They're going to kill us!" after I put the vegetables down for her.

She said, "Your mother was a baby in my mother's arms." She said, "I get out of breath now when I eat. Jule says I'm not the same since I was sick. He says to me, You've changed."

"You haven't changed," I said.

She said, "They had the wagon loaded. They had the cow. You know they had to take the cow to give the children milk to drink. They were going to hide! To hide! To hide in the woods! And then Jule said, I've got to go!

"Everything was loaded. They said, Hurry! They're coming! They're going to kill us! But Jule said, I've got to go! So they said, Do it! Do it! Hurry! So then Jule said, But I need *the pot*!"

"He said that?" I said. "I never heard that story. Does my mother know that story?"

My aunt smiled, which I took then to be no. And my mother wasn't there, so I couldn't rush to her, I couldn't tell her, Do you know the story about your family? How you were going to be killed? How Uncle Jule stopped everything to go?

Uncle Jule appeared then. He was wearing a white golf hat.

My aunt said, *"You could put it in your hat."* She said that to Jule. I don't remember why she said that—*You could put it in your hat.*

He must have said something first to her about her vegetables—could he take home what she wasn't going to eat? Maybe that was it—but it doesn't matter.

Uncle Jule was blinking and smiling when she said, *You could put it in your hat.* He was blinking faster than anyone needs to blink.

Cauliflower was what my aunt left on her plate. It looked to me like some bleached-out tree.

24

TEN FEET
FROM IT

His body shifts and gets closer to me in a shady part of our house where hardly any natural light can get to, unless a bathroom door is open fully. At no time during this is he more than two or three feet away from me, and always he keeps turning to me so I can see how he is, not to prove anything to me. He is not the kind to do that. I am.

He is my son, one of them.

My other son broke down for me later in this day, my husband the same, a few days ago, my brother later in this day. My mother said to me, "I am not with it," just after we both witnessed my brother.

I can put the sight of any of them up in front of myself again anytime I want to: my son in grief because I would not believe that he really is; my other son the same; my husband, when he told me, "That broke the ice," after what I had said to him—whatever it was; my brother, as he was telling me his life is at stake.

My mother, her grief is the most overwhelming.

She was sitting with her Old Testament which has such tissue-thin pages and she was making the pages make a noise when I found her.

The biggest, broadest window of her house was in front of her, where she was sitting with the open book. I have the same dark red leather-bound version of the text.

I said to my mother, "Let me kiss you." I was up close to her, my hands on her forearms to get closer to her, but I did not get closer. For some reason she was standing at that time, perhaps to let me try, and then she was down, sitting at the desk which had been my desk when I was a girl.

She was looking at the shake-shingled roof, at the plum tree, at the trees all pushed together beyond it, at the violent plunging-down that our land takes below that window where one of my sons killed himself, because he was trying to keep my other sons from killing themselves, just about ten feet from the plum tree. He was shouting at those boys, or he was talking softly to those boys, who were talking softly to him, so all of them had to lean so far over to hear what they had to hear, so one of them could die.

It is just a sight with the body of my mother in front of it.

26

I can refer to the window glass. I can refer to the sky which might as well be the sea.

I go down the stairs of my mother's house, satisfied and slowly.

I cannot get a sight up in front of me now of little boys or of grown-ups together, so that I can hear what they are saying, so that I would want to repeat what it was they were saying, so that what they have said would change everything once and for all.

DROPPING
THE MASTERS

There was a clatting sound, for all this kissing,
for all this copulation. My boys could get
those Masters of the Universe up and onto the
dresser top in one swoop up—*a kiss to the bride! a kiss to
the bride!*—it was the only way they got them married,
the way my youngest boy had decided they should get
them married. One swoop down and then they could
rock a pair and make those Masters copulate just as long
as they wanted them to. Until I let my boys see me so
that I saw the faces of I'm hot and I'm caught, and I saw

the faces of this has got to stop—that's the way I saw them when they were stopping, when a hand was up with a Master, when a boy the height of our dog begging was up on his knees like he was handing out a bone.

I was going nowhere after I stopped them, just down the hall toward the bathroom, just stuck almost at the end of the top of our house so that of course I didn't want to stay there where I had no business being or intention, where I felt stupid and strange almost in the bathroom. Now their door was shut so that I could hear the sound of them, but I could get no meaning. I could hear rough scrubbing and more clatting and not know anything about it at all. But I was back in front of the shut door of their room and there was nowhere else I wanted to be more than watching again or just to know what they knew—to know everything about what they knew and so that is where I stood.

So then I opened their door.

But this time the stopping was not like the stopping before, it was an altogether different kind of stopping. This was how dare you with the Masters being deeply ground down I thought maybe so they would break because these Masters break.

What I got to see then was the sluggishness of let's do another thing—the turning away and then the boys hopping the Masters and then dropping them.

These Masters weren't broken, they were only done—and my boys were walking out on me, finished.

THERE SHOULD
BE NOTHING
REMARKABLE

T here should be nothing remarkable about reading a lovey-dovey Hallmark card out loud to your old father, nothing, please bear with me, as bad as the hope that you are being smuggled into the United States, so that you can be a restaurant hostess, and then you end up in a brothel, as a slave, in New York, San Francisco, or Colorado—or nothing, let me go further boldly, as remarkable as the difference between announcing this notion of extreme affection with words which are not your own, and the fate of a poor girl, which might be the same, if you would indulge me wildly, as the difference between a duck! which my father asked me about when I was a girl.

Perhaps it wasn't his own question—original with him—"What's the difference between a duck?"—but I worked on it as if it were, not even hopelessly. Right away, in my mind, I'd search those webbed feet, or my eyes would rise up the white neck of the duck, ever so slowly, alert for the presto change-o, so I could be the first one to tell him what the difference was. I am sure I tried to tell him. I don't remember the words.

I have seen the photograph of this act, of my father waiting for me. The envelope is cocked, the card is on the way out, my hand is on it, and I am positively demure with my eyes cast shyly down. I think he waits the way the beauty would wait—imagining—"This way," her own elegance, "please," so correctly distant, so that those prospective eaters could worship her from any distance, before, during, or after being led off.

Speaking for myself, the worst fate I can imagine would be a restaurant job of any kind. I don't think my attitude about that will change, ever, unless I have become near dead with hunger—wasted—but in that case, I could not get a real job. You must look the part of a worker to get yourself paid, and isn't money very much to the point? or what is it which is the root of all evil—how you sign yourself away? physical beauty? *You be my slave*—you throw yourself at somebody's feet—*I am yours*—it is so cozy, what I have done. It is my idea of family.

31

BABY

Nobody was getting up close to me, whispering, "Do you get a lot of sex?" Nobody was making my mouth fall open by running his finger up and down my spine, or anything like that, or talking dirty about dirty pictures and did I have those or anything like those, so I could tell him what I keep— what I have been keeping for so long in my bureau drawer underneath my cable-knit pink crew—so I could tell him what I count on happening to me every time I take it out from under there. Because it was a baby party for one thing, so we had cone paper hats and blowers, so we had James Beard's mother's cake with turquoise icing, and it was all done up inside with scarlet and pea-green squiggles, and the baby got toys.

Nobody was saying, "Everybody has slept with my wife, because everybody has slept with everybody, so why don't we sleep together?" so I could say at last, "Yes, please. Thank you for thinking of me." I would be polite.

Just as it was nothing out of the ordinary when the five-year-old slugged the eleven-year-old on the back and they kept on playing, looking as if they could kill for a couple of seconds. We didn't know why. And then the baby cried in a bloodthirsty way.

My husband sat stony-faced throughout. I don't think he moved from his chair once. What the fuck was wrong with him? He left the party early, without me; he said to get a little—I don't know how he was spelling it—I'll spell it *peace*.

I spoke to a mustached man right after my husband left. He was the first man all night I had tried to speak to. I know he loves sports. I said to him, "I think sports are wonderful. There are triumphs. It is so exciting. But first, you have to know what is going on."

Then my boy was whining, "Mom, I want to go home." He was sounding unbearably tired.

The baby's aunt said she'd take us. She didn't mind. She had to back up her car on the icy drive. She said, "I don't know how we'll get out of here," when we got into the car. "The windows are all fogged up." She said, "I don't think I can do it." She opened the window and poked her head out. She said, "I don't think so."

When she closed the window, we went backward

terrifically fast. I don't know how she knew when to spin us around into the street. It was like being in one of those movies I have seen the previews for. It was like watching one of those faces on those people who try to give you the willies. It was like that, watching her—while she tried to get us out.

CLOUD

How it was in the aftermath of it, was that her body was in the world, not how it had ever been in the world before, in her little room or in *their* rooms—the people who owned the rooms—or at least were managing the rooms, their hallways, or the stairwell, which was not hers either, that she went through and through and through. A man laughed at her for what she had said, and then someone had brought her to this bed.

35

She looked at the bed stacked high with so many coats and she decided, It all stops here.

She was clearing up to be helpful before she left, steering herself, when she saw her purse go flying and then it fell down into a corner.

She was down too, walloped by a blow, by some man, and she thought, I understand. She thought, This is easy. She thought, It's as easy as my first fuck. She had opened up so wide.

In the street, crossing to go home, her purse swung on her arm by its strap. She thought the dark air was so soft to walk through.

And for all that the girl knew there had not been a jot on her when she looked—no proof JACK WAS HERE! on her skin in red and in bright green ink, with any exclamation she could see, about them doing things, or about any one of them being of the opinion that her tits sucked.

And for the rest of her life, the girl, the woman, she never made a mark on anyone either that proved anything absolutely for certain, that she could ever see, about what she had done at any time, and this does not break her heart.

FORTY
THOUSAND
DOLLARS

When she said forty thousand dollars for her
diamond ring, where did I go with this fact?
I followed right along with her, hoping,
hoping for a ring like hers for myself, because of what I
believe deep down, that she is so safe because she has
her ring, that she is as safe as her ring is big—and so is
her entire family—her husband who gave her the ring,
all of her children—and no one has ever tried to talk me
out of believing this fact, because I would never speak
of it, that the entire quality of her life is totally secure

37

because of the size of that ring—that the ring is a complete uplift—that every single thing else about her is up to the standard the size of her ring sets, such as even her denim espadrilles, which I love, which she was wearing the day she was talking to me, or her gray hair pulled back, so serene, so that she is adored, so that she is everlastingly loved by her husband, and why not?— just look at her!—and she is loved by her children, and by everyone like me who has ever laid eyes on her and her ring.

She was waggling it, which I loved her to do, because I loved to see it move, to see it do anything at all, and she said, "I make my meat loaf with it." She said, "I like that about it, too," and I saw the red meat smears she was talking about, smearing up the ring the way they would do, the bread all swollen up all over it, all over the ring part and the jewel. I saw my whole recipe on that ring.

She said, "It goes along with me to take out my garbage, and I like that," and I saw what she meant, how it would take out the garbage if it were taking it out with me, how it would go down with me, down the steps and out the back door—the ring part of the ring buried in the paper of the bag—and the dumping we would do together of the bag into the sunken can, before the likelihood of a break or a tear, or maybe I'd have to step on top of a whole heap of bags that was already down in there and then stamp on the top of the heap myself, to get it all deep down, to get the lid on with the ring on.

She said, "I never knew I was going to get anything like it. All that Harry said was, 'We'll need a wheelbar-row for you *and* the ring when you get it.' A wheelbar-

38

row!" she said. "But now don't worry," she said to me. "You'll get one someday, too. Somebody will die," she said, "then you'll get yours—" Which is exactly what happened—I never had to pay money for mine, and mine ended up to be even bigger than hers. "This much bigger—" I showed her with two fingers that I almost put together, the amount, which is probably at least another carat more, but mine is stuck inside an old setting and cannot be measured. That was the day I walked behind her, that I showed her, that I walked with her to her car when she was leaving my house.

The rings were of no account outside, when we were saying goodbye, when we were outside my house going toward the back side of her car, because we were not looking at the rings then. The heels of her denim espadrilles, which matched her long, swinging skirt, were going up and down, so was her strong ponytail, and her shoulders, and I wanted to go along with her to wherever she was going.

And then the sense I had of not being able to stay behind her—of not being able to see myself in my own clothes walking away—the sense I had that I was not where I was, that I could not possibly follow in my own footsteps, was gone.

PORNOGRAPHY

I just had a terrible experience—I'm sorry. I was yelling at my boy, "Don't you ever!" I saw this crash. I saw this little old man. The door of the car opened and I saw this little old man tottering out. Somebody said, "I saw him!" The same somebody said, "He's already hit two cars."

There was this kid. He wasn't a kid. He was about nineteen. He was screaming and screaming on a bicycle.

Then I saw him, the kid, on the stretcher.

That little old man did more for me than any sex has ever done for me. I got these shudders.

The same thing with another kid—this one tiny, the same thing, on a stretcher, absolutely quiet in a playground, and I was far enough away so that I did not know what had happened. I never found out. Same thing, shudders that I tried to make last, because I thought it would be wonderful if they would last for at least the four blocks it took me to get home and they were lasting and then I saw two more boys on their bicycles looking to get hit, not with any menace like they wanted to *do* anything to me, because I wasn't even over the white crossing line, not yet, and the only reason I saw either one of them was because I was ready to turn and I was looking at the script unlit yellow neon *l* on the cleaner's marquee which was kitty-corner to me, when just off that *l* I saw the red and the orange and my driver's leg struck up and down hard on the brake without my thinking, even though I think I was ready to go full out at that time, because where was I going, anyway? back home to my boy?

My car was rocking, the nose of it, against the T-shirts of those boys, first the red one, and then the orange one, and they each of them, they looked me in the eye.

Back home, my boy, he's only five, he's going to show me, making himself into a bicycle streak down our drive, heading, he says, for my mother's house, heading for that dangerous curve where so many horrible accidents have happened or have almost happened. What I did was yell at him DON'T YOU DO THAT! but he was already off, and then this goddamn little thing, this animal, this tiny chipmunk thing races with all its

41

stripes right up at me, but not all the way *to* me, and then the thing, it whips around and runs away, like right now with my boy—I can't—there is no other way to put it—I *can't come*.

HERE'S
ANOTHER
ENDING

This time my story has a foregone conclusion. It is true also.

After I tell the story, I say, "You could start a religion based on a story like that—couldn't you?"

The story begins with my idea of a huge dog—a Doberman—which is to me an emblem—cruel, not lovable.

The dog is a household pet in a neighborhood such as mine, with houses with backyards which abut.

The huge dog is out and about when it should not be. It should never be.

When the dog returns to its owners, it is carrying in its mouth a dirty dead rabbit.

The dog's owners exclaim—one of them does—"The neighbor's rabbit! He's killed it!" The dog's owners conclude, "We must save our dog's reputation at all costs." They think, Our dog is in jeopardy.

The dog's owners shampoo the dead rabbit and dry it with a hair dryer. At night, they sneak the rabbit back into their neighbor's yard, into its cage.

The morning of the following day, the dog's owners hear a shriek from the rabbit owners' yard. They think, Oh! The dead rabbit has been discovered! They rush to see what's what.

One of the rabbit's owners—the father in the family—is holding the limp, white rabbit up in the air. He says to the dog's owners, "We buried her two days ago!"

The dog's owners explain nothing. They won't, but not because they are ashamed of themselves.

There is another, more obvious reason.

MY FEMALE
HONOR IS
OF A TYPE

I did some V last night of a kind I have not done
before. I gave myself permission. I said to myself
calmly in my mind—on this occasion I will give
you permission to do the following—listen carefully to
yourself: you are allowed to cut up your husband's
money which is on his bureau top, just the single bills,
there are not too many of them; cut up his business card
which is in his card case, and then cut up a folded piece
of paper—you do not know what it is. There, you are
cutting paper.

He gave me permission when he saw me, even, even when he saw me leafing through big bills with the scissors and the card case, flipping to choose, and sorting the paper, the opportunity for cutting.

The occasion for this V which I permitted and which my husband permitted was anger of a type.

I said to her, *"You should fear for your life!"* Tonight I said, "Tell *them* you feared for it!" Whereas my husband would have left. He would have walked out mildly and back to home.

They say so, and then their head is in your vision, only their spooky eyes, or their bony nose shaking, not even their mouth is in your vision because you are too close, maybe some of this someone's platinum hairs mixed up with silver and brown and white, and pale pale yellow hairs, antiseptic hairs is what I call it, clean out of grease or refuse.

But not the hairs on *her* head, not the crisply cut card with the credentials she put for me to see, hairy letters on a hairy card, the card of someone who ran the whole show, that I could not even see the name, because of hair, nor did I want to.

"You've got what you wanted!" she said, so that all the hairs were not enough hairs, or the telephone in the bag she gave me, the black phone. All the hairs were not like the hairs on *her* head which she pinned up or she pulled down which she waved, which she lustered fully out. All the little rings on the black cord to put your finger in, to hold your finger, all the little rings that stretch to ringlets, all the twirlies.

We left. It was between her and her. The husband and the mild-mannered boy behind her, and the husband did not play key roles. We ran the show and when

46

I left something did die, a little something, and later on she will know something teeny keeled. I took that teeny thing, and the fat phone in the fat bag. I took the teeny tiny pathetic, that can climb in between hairs all by itself, that can lay down their eggs to hatch.

I would not do murder for a phone. I would do it for hair.

GLASS OF
FASHION

My mother touched the doctor's hair—"Your hair—" she said. I was looking at the doctor's eyes—black and as sad as any eyes I had ever looked at—doleful, mournful—but I thought she is hard-hearted too, this doctor. She must be hard-hearted. Hard-hearted is part of her job. It has to be.

The doctor's hair was full and long and down, kinky and wavy and black. My mother's hair is short and white and kinky and wavy and I could see why my mother was admiring her hair. I was admiring the doctor's body in her jeans. She had what I thought was a girlish and perfect form in her jeans, an enviable form.

There were four of us backed up to the large window at the end of the hall, because I had said, "Let's go over to the window to talk"—my mother, my sister, and me, and this very young woman doctor with black hair, black eyes, and jeans on.

We were at the window at the hospital, at the end of a hall, down from what was left of my father. We were getting the report on my father, because I had said to the doctor, "Tell us."

Maybe the doctor was a little ashamed too, or belligerent, when she was telling us. Her eyes had such a film over them, so that they sparkled when she spoke of his cerebellum, about his brain stem, about the size of his cortical function. She said, "He doesn't know who he is. He does not know who he once was. He does not feel grief or frustration. He does not know who you are." What I was envying then were the doctor's legs in her jeans. "Maybe—" I said, "you know, maybe—he had such a big brain before—it is just possible," I said, "that even if his brain has been ravaged, he is still a smart enough person."

The doctor did not say anything about that. No one did.

Chrissy, one of Dad's day-shift nurses, was coming along then toward us. Her glasses are the kind my sister will not wear. She will not get glasses like that. My mother will not either. A serious person's glasses—even if Chrissy is only just a nurse, even if she cannot explain very much about the brain, because she explained to me she has been out of school for too long—I can tell she is serious, that she is serious about me too. If she

49

were a man I would call what we have shared romantic love—we have shared so much, so often here—talking about my father with feeling. If she were a man—even if she couldn't remember half of what she had learned about the brain—even if she had forgotten it all—*no*— if she had forgotten it all, totally, I don't think I'd want to spend the time of day in her presence. She would disgust me, if she were a man like that. So when she called us, when she said, "Your father—" and then when I called "Dad! Dad!" from the—and it sounded even to me as if I expected he would rise up—then I was ready for what I was feeling when I touched his forehead—which was still warm. His mouth was open. The front of the lower row of his teeth was showing. The teeth had never looked, each of them, so terribly small. Some of his teeth were the last things on my father that I ever touched.

PASSAGE
OF THE SOUL

S he said, "Don't get excited," to the scar-faced
man.
He was excited, more like agitated. I remembered lots of men I have been with being like that. It
was a worry. Maybe he was someone who shouldn't
have been out.

She said, "We don't have to stay," and then I saw him
in the snack line, way behind me, stuck in the heavy
crowd, from where another woman's voice scolded
somebody, "You had to pick the most popular picture of

all the pictures!" Next, I found my husband. I always can. He goes ahead without me for the seats.

We hardly speak in theaters, waiting. I twisted myself around to watch a girl behind us feed her boyfriend one popped kernel of corn, and then kiss him, and I saw him touch her breast, because we had to wait and wait, even for the previews to begin. I decided her boyfriend was no one I would want touching from, and I didn't flinch; he did, when I watched him watch me make my decision. It was as though he couldn't believe it, that he couldn't believe it—that I would judge him with such haste.

I would have run off with the character named Tom in the movie, so that they could see once and for all, as he put it to the woman, how they would be together, away from all of *this*. She ended up unappealing. She must have had a moment of horror—the actress—when she first saw herself like that.

At one time, seven years earlier in the movie, it seemed the whole audience had heaved a huge sigh watching her—not me, I just listened—I never would want to let on what I was thinking, You are so bold and lucky, when she dropped the prophylactics into her purse before she went out, and I was eager to see what would happen.

There are so many other things to recount about that movie. I left the theater with our balled-up empty popcorn bucket in my hand, to throw it away at home: that's what I was thinking about on the way to our car, that I'd have to hold it in my hand, which I did, feeling it, the squashed-up waxy rim of the bottom of it, all the way home; that somehow I had ended up like this. I had missed, just to begin with, the opportunity to throw it away inside the theater.

When we were getting ready for bed, I got myself into sort of a state. I saw that my husband was wearing what I considered to be the trousers of my pajamas—I have only one pair—which I had planned to put on, which had belonged to him once long ago, it's true, but hadn't he given them to me?

"What do you think you're doing?" I asked him. "I don't get it. What are you doing?"

I saw him, his body, his bare chest, which is sleek and perfectly formed by my standards—he was pulling down and folding the spread of our bed, in those cotton striped trousers. My husband is so graceful, how he moved around the foot of the bed was so graceful, how he gently, carefully folded.

Oh, he gave me back the trousers; so then we slept.

I didn't know what the issue was.

When the ringing of the telephone woke us in the night, we both knew what it could mean—everybody does—or it could have been just somebody borderline, wanting to hear the sound of anyone in a fright. That's what it was that time.

More will happen.

It will be stunning.

It's what I'm waiting for.

Some people are lucky—just walking, just going around, when you look at them.

ORIGINAL
BELIEF

I was thinking, Would someone else's husband—*not mine!*—would Nancy Harp's husband want the woman?

To make a judgment I thought, do *I* want her?

Oh, yes!

When her cutaway shirt buckled and slid, I saw the perky, side-view form of her naked breast.

Nancy Harp's husband, I thought, must be beside himself all the time with this woman—and she was straight-legged, and she intended for her face to be pretty, and it was!

The Harps' whole kitchen, where I met the woman—
their Formica getting all the sun—the wood floor, when
I looked down, I thought, *It must be cherry!* was driving
me crazy.

Oh, I knew the woman was a do-nothing maid. Her
employer, Nancy—and Nancy is my friend—told me
she does not allow this maid to cook. Nancy said she
told the maid, "I do that!" when the maid had said, "I
could do that."

While I watched her, the maid went this way or she
went that way, ever so lightly on her bare feet. She was
not upset. But, she may have considered the possi-
bilities to share with me, because neither my son, nor
any member of the Harp family, was on the premises,
and they should have been when I got there.

At the stairs, she called, *"Davey!"*

It could be a blessing that I was not worried, to not
know what she did not understand, because there was
the problem of the language problem.

She did say, "Who are you?" so I said, "The mom."

I underscored *naughty* about Davey because he
should have been there at the Harps'. He said he would.

I was safe and she was safe, including Davey, with
my *naughty.*

Something about cute and safe means the same thing
to me. But I didn't stop there. I got myself degraded.

THE SPOILS

The girl did not know why the boys were looking for her when she was spoiling herself—
what to her was a spoiling—why the boys
inside from the garden party in the hall of her house
were banging on the locked door to get to her. She knew
who they were. They were her guests.

The girl had not yet spoiled herself—but when she
was full of it—full to bursting—she broke out of there.
She broke out of there to get to those boys.

Now none of them had to break in or out of anywhere
because now they were meeting in the hall of her house.

With one stroke in the hall of her house, for those boys, slipping suddenly out, she left her spoils for them—neatly coiled. She looked to see.

It was the tops of their heads, the three tops of their heads that she saw, because those boys were looking to see too.

Then the girl was going back out to more guests—to the garden, to the garden party, and she was going on, back out to where she was the smallest daughter of the host and hostess of the garden party, the party which was for every aunt and uncle and cousin and for all friends.

This garden was full of it for her. She could name the flowers in the garden. She could name the flowers that had been in the garden. She could name the flowers that would come into the garden.

Her largest uncle was scolding in the garden—her uncle with the ring of hair around his skin-topped head—like teeth biting neat bites, she thought, all the way around his skin-top. She heard him. He said *You are so spoiled* with his head hanging over his daughter, so that to the girl watching, his head was where his daughter's head should have been, and the daughter and the uncle were stuck on the stony path between the hedges that led to the steps up back into the house.

When the uncle said *You are so spoiled*, neither of them moved, and those hedges, those big green hedges were brushing them.

Then the uncle's daughter was going up the steps, leaving the uncle, because, the girl thought, because *You are so spoiled* means you must leave.

That girl will meet the boys inside there when she gets inside there, the girl watching thought.

And the girl watched the girl disappear.

INTERCOURSE

At the post office the woman finally got a good long look at the monster, a stare. She was breathing the same air, not as before, deprived.

When she had first sighted the monster, this woman had not been sure whether or not to trust her instinct.

Was it a monster?

What it was was a monstrous posture she had seen, and the hair on top of the head was heaped so that it appeared as a bulge of hair, with far too much hair coming down at the side, so as to be an abnormal amount. Otherwise, the form of the monster was spindly. It was a small-sized monster.

The eyes were pale turquoise. The facial skin was milky milky white. The nose was a short, finely shaped nose. The mouth was full-lipped, painted coral. The hair was the woman's favorite color hair—cinnamon color. The voice was girl-like when the woman heard it. The black-inked handwriting on the brown-paper-wrapped package was indecipherable from the distance it was observed from, but it was a curvaceous handwriting. The high-heeled shoes with ankle straps were made of metallic gold leather. The purse was like bronze.

OK, the emergence of this bombshell has gone on long enough for me. Occasionally I select a man, but my preference is for women who could easily steal away my beloved husband who is not taboo.

Carnality is common in rude society. The incarnation is temporary or permanent.

OK FOR
PEOPLE

It was dark outside, a wicked dark, on an early January evening, about six o'clock—but there were just the two of us in my house at the time, which could have meant that it was peaceful in my kitchen with my mother.

She would say she was returning, but she would not say from where. She did say she was trying to get to her house, which is not far from here by car. Her car was parked in our drive.

From my kitchen in her mink coat she called the

police. My mother wanted my brother or the police. She would not say what it was about before the phoning, first to find my brother.

She looked desperate before the phoning, or as if she were being pursued by someone who desperately loved her. I was wishing that's what it was. I wasn't pretending that's what it was. I was wishing that she was being pursued by someone who desperately loved her and that this circumstance was unspeakable, that it was trouble that could not be shared with anyone possibly faint-hearted, which she thought I might be—that it was trouble, this unspeakable circumstance which then pressed at her and the phone receiver against the wall of my kitchen, her face to the wall phone in her mink coat, and then the trouble kept pressing at her, so that she was hunched over my kitchen counter in the coat, which had such a sheen that she had to tell me that, no, it wasn't new—when she was listening to the ringing, trying to get through.

When she did get through, not to my brother, but to the police, she had a way with her voice, for what she was saying to them, that I have never heard her use in front of me before. I thought that her voice could make a policeman think he should rush to her, if he wanted to share something sort of fun and safe, when he was slitting, as she had asked him to do, one of her screen doors, so that he could break open the locked latch of it, so that she could get into her house.

She would not speak of any trouble in front of me— not the real trouble—how could she ever?—which is that nobody can get my dead father here again with us from the dead, alive, nor should we want them to, because he was a dangerous man.

So my mother had put herself into the hands of the police, so that everything that had to be done would be done for her.

Her coat fanned as she was leaving. It skimmed and slipped and slid above her black leather boots—the strung-together pelts and skins—whatever they are—were dazzling.

So then she was going out the door and everything was OK for people who will lie down and be dead—not like my father—who passed it down as a legacy—"Don't confuse me with the facts," because some people never lie down to take it—it is not their nature.

My mother—leaving here to return—was so full of something akin to swagger, I wanted to yell out after her, "Knock 'em dead!" Surely there is a way to murder someone who is already dead if that is what you must do to get them off of your back, so you can live a little.

The mystery: How were the screen doors latched and locked, when there was no one inside my mother's house?—that was not the mystery.

My mother was the one who had latched and locked the screen doors, which she has been doing ever since my father died. A garage door opening device, when it can open, because it cannot always, lets her get back in.

The mystery: My father was discovered with a puncture wound on the left side of his neck and a large cut below his right jaw. He bled to death.

Even in the wild, an expert told us, dogs will attack to assert themselves, not to kill. It doesn't matter how lovable and loyal the family dog is.

The mystery: Which one of us reached my father before the dog?

62

LIFE
AFTER
DEATH

H e had on a bright yellow shirt and there were objects in there with him that were rapturously green, things in the light.

Then there was somebody with him who was on the move, boringly, and who was boringly talking.

This was the one she stopped from talking, a larger-than-life type, with jeans torn-up at the knee, and it was true he was talking about nothing when he stopped talking.

His legs were mighty legs. His head was a mighty

head. His nose was probably a mighty nose, if she had seen it. There were some sickening greenish and yellowish and reddish strings that whipped around together, some way, around him, dragging off of something on him, that was coming apart on him, that whirled, before he made his exit, while she was thinking, IT'S ENOUGH!

He got killed by her because he was in-between. She knew all about in-between, all about it—she knew enough about it so that what she knew would last longer than she was going to live for.

Afterward, she remembered how once a strict authority had told her, "You are in for some adventures."

One adventure had been to see the configuration, and the black and the dull pink colors of the male sex organs. One adventure was watching the man cover his organs up, by pulling up his blue jeans, and zipping the organs up inside of the blue jeans. One adventure was hearing the man she had killed tell her what an authority had told him about what she and he could do together, on and on.

One adventure she won't have. She won't ever know what happens if she does not do what she wants to do. Life afterward is not anything like three, stuck-in-the-mud people, up against one another, and she is the one up on the back end of another woman, while a man is all boarded up onto the back end of her, while the man is being mindful—full only of her.

SCREAMING

I thought she had grabbed her whole pearl necklace in a fist to stop it at her throat so that we could speak, because it had been crashing into itself, back and forth across her breast, as she was moving toward me.

"Your dog Heather"—was all I could think to say to her—"I still remember your story about Heather, your dog, and about your daughter coming down the stairs in the black wig."

"That was Heidi," she said.

"Your daughter is Heidi?"

"No," she said, "that's the dog."

"Oh, and she's not living," I said as she let the pearls go and they fell back down against her chest.

"That's right," she said. "Heather is. Heather's a better name—that's why you remember Heather. Heather is—" and she rolled her eyes so that I would know that I should have remembered Heather.

We did not talk about Heidi anymore that night, and I did not bring her up for conversation, because I did not have to. I spoke to her husband instead.

Still, I remembered how when the daughter was coming down the stairs in the black wig, wearing the kimono, Heidi ran away. I want to say that Heidi ran away screaming when she saw the daughter—but Heidi is the dog. She was a dog.

For the sake of conversation, when her husband and I saw a woman neither of us knew, I said, "I bet she's not afraid of a living soul." I said it because the woman had obviously done her hair all by herself for this gala—just stuck bobby pins you could see into her white hair, just worn an old, out-of-fashion cotton dress.

I told the husband I'd like to shake that woman's hand and ask her if it was true what I had guessed.

I was considering it, getting up close. I wondered would she get scared or what she would do—what I would do.

"What about that one there?" her husband asked.

That one there was a woman who was trying to get back behind my husband. The woman was wincing as if she had just done something awful.

"A gambling problem—that's what she has," I said. But that wasn't sordid enough. So then I said, "I don't have a clue."

"Now me," the husband said. "Do me."

"You," I said, "you are hardworking. You are—"

"No," he said, "*not that*—" The man looked frightened. He looked ready to hear what I would say as if I really knew.

Then someone was at my back, tugging at my hair, moving it. I felt a mouth was on the nape of my neck. It was a kiss.

I did not have the faintest idea who would want to do that to me. There was not a soul.

When I saw him, when I turned, his head was still hung down low from kissing me. He was full of shame.

Thank God I did not know who he was.

I kept my face near his. I liked the look of him.

I was praying he would do something more to me. Anything.

HOPE

She had the proof to prove it to me that her dying
father's idiot wife, who was not her mother, was
a real idiot. My friend said that this woman
spelled the word *wife* W-I-L-F on the hospital informa-
tion request form, so that my friend had to do everything for her father, because he said to her, "You have to
help me!"

She had taken care of the funeral arrangements, and
her father was not dead yet.

My father's dying was not planned for so carefully by
his daughter, and it is over with. He's dead.

We had appointments—my friend and I—at the exact same time, and if it had not been for her arriving, just when she did, at the third-floor hallway of the Professional Medical Arts Building, I would have left after arriving there first, all alone, and knocking and knocking and hammering and yelling at the office door, and twisting and twisting the doorknob, and listening with disbelief to the unanswered ringing of the telephone inside.

We were well along in our discussion, comforting one another about our fathers, we had even compared our teeth, when our dentist arrived, his staff, his hygienist, and so forth.

My friend had told me, by then, how awful her father was—she had proof—and so had I told her that my father wasn't that awful, but that he might as well have been—because I had hated him as much as she had hated hers by the end.

Once inside the office, we discovered that nobody expected us to sit in the same chair, or to lie down together in it with our mouths open while they yapped at us, while *she*— The hygienist had the nerve to ask a question I could not answer. I was not able to speak and she knew it.

It was unbelievable, unbelievable that a daughter such as me, whose father had been so loving to her all of her life, who wanted to tell me what I needed to know anytime that I needed to know, that I should deliberately ask my father a question after the doctors had rendered him positively without the power of speech, that I should ask him a question, and then act as if it were a matter of life or death that my question had no answer.

Every time I do not know what else to think, I go

back to how my hands were grabbing onto my father's ankles or onto his toes. I felt so incredibly nervy. He was down in his bed. I was at the end of it. My father put his head forward toward me, crazy to tell me the most essential thing I will ever need to know.

THE
DIVINE
RIGHT

W hat your king did—" she was saying to the Dutchman.

"King? Do you even know the country? You don't even know which country. We have no king," the Dutchman said.

"No king? Your consort—the queen's consort?" she said.

"You mean the prince?"

"Bern—Bern—what he did was terrible, taking all that money. Why did he take the money? He doesn't need the money. He's married to the richest woman in the world."

The Dutchman laughed. "The richest woman in the world? Do you think so? Well, I hope so."

"Doesn't she own most of Fifth Avenue, along with that other queen? the Queen of England?"

"Well, I don't know," the Dutchman said.

"You don't know? You don't think it was a bad thing what he did, taking that money?"

"No, none of us do," the Dutchman said. "We all like him very much. The money was offered, and he took it. It's no big deal."

"Well, here we all thought it was terrible. I thought it was. I hated him for it. I felt so sorry for the queen."

"What I can't get over," the Dutchman said, "in your country, are all those rich people's names plastered all over your museums—those plaques. Rich people in our country would never do that. They would be so embarrassed to do that."

"They would be?" she asked.

"Yes. They would never do that."

"Well, I wouldn't really do it either," she said. "Maybe a tiny tag that I had donated this or that, but not a huge plaque announcing a whole wing or anything like that. That would be embarrassing. It would be so obvious."

"What you were after?" the Dutchman laughed. "Are you very rich?"

"What?" she said.

"*You*, are you *rich*?" the Dutchman asked.

"I suppose that I am," Mrs. Osborne said. "Will you excuse me, please?"

In the mirror of her host's bathroom she saw her

small oval face and her large earrings, each earring the size of one of her ears, rectangles of lapis lazuli framed in gold. She was embarrassed by the size of the earrings. She took the earrings off. She slipped them into her purse.

She was embarrassed by the size of her purse, the leather was too luxuriantly soft. She remembered the cost of the purse. She remembered the cost of the earrings.

She found Mr. Osborne in the host's kitchen, pouring himself a glass of wine. "I want to go home," she whispered.

"You tired?" Mr. Osborne asked.

"No," she answered, "I am not tired."

She held her gloved hands up in front of her as they walked to their car. She thought her gloves were a gaudy shade of green. She remembered the cost of the gloves. It would not bother her never to wear them again.

Sliding inside their car, she was afraid suddenly they were being watched. In this neighborhood, for the price of the car, they could be killed. They could be killed anywhere.

Mr. Osborne petted his wife's arm, before he turned the key to begin the drive home. He was petting the sleek seal fur of her coat. One of his hands, the glowing flesh of it, was all that she could see. She was frantic. She thought, What if I am really adored too—if it is true! She remembered.

POWER

How do they do it? She cannot bend her legs. Here I go, I must see him propping up her legs some way onto his shoulders, or with some contraption that they have had to devise, or do they simply put a bunch of something under her hips, or does he get into her from behind when they are lying down? or something else so obvious, but I don't know. She sits in his lap in a chair? and does it hurt her, because it is awkward? or do they even bother to try, because it is never fun? Or does she do it for him some way with her mouth? How would she do it that way?

74

Her legs shine under the mesh nylon of her hose. I look right at her legs when she says, "Oh, these legs." I do not know these people, the husband, and the wife, or the driver of this car that we are all paying to please get us home. At least, I know I have been away.

I do not know where to begin with this injury—with the sharpness of her nose which seems to solve something, the brightness of the light shooting off from her lacquered cane, or her laughing many more times than once, so that her husband said to her, "What is the matter?" or her ever-constant soft drawing up of a breath through her nose—once, then twice, and then pause—the sense of the stupid loss of time, that for once did not matter to me.

I thought, Let us keep on at this looking for the house they are looking for. It does not matter that the driver of the car cannot find it. Once I thought that.

She said to me, "I did not mean to throw my cane at you."

The door of the car had opened, the cane had been flung by someone onto the seat toward me, then her body. She had flung her body onto the back seat the wrong way—flat out and on her back—because of her problem, her big problem, her husband's bigger problem, their terrific problem.

She said, "No, this is not it," whenever the driver beamed a light on a house.

I said, "It is so dark." Finally, I said angrily, "Is this even the street?"

The driver said, "Yes!" and then I saw LOCUST in block black letters on a white sign on the corner at just that moment when the driver spoke.

She said, "No, this is not it."

When finally it was the house—those relatives, those

people up there who came out onto that cement porch, who maybe call themselves friends, were not happy enough to receive their guests. That chirruping woman with her arms around the other woman didn't fool me. Nobody fooled me, but probably somebody was being fooled.

At least I knew where I lived. I could say to the driver, "Straight east now, and then left at the light." I could say it and say it and keep on with it, even with a righteous sense of anger—thank God—with a sense of—*You listen to me! This is how you get somewhere!*

But all this is not about failed love.

Somebody please tell me that this is all about something else entirely which is more important.

Somebody smarter and dearer than I, be the one available for my best, my most tenderest embrace when I have been convinced by you.

I could be a believer.

WHAT IS IT WHEN GOD SPEAKS?

This was the house which once inspired a sister of one of the guests to declare, "People kill for this."

That's where the guests were on the perfect afternoon, not the sister.

It was a shame the afternoon became evening before the guests had to leave, not that anything was less lovely because it was evening.

There was a tender quality to the lack of light on the screened-in porch where they all were sitting, as there was also a tender quality to the small girl too old to be in the highchair, but she was not too large for it. The girl had insisted the highchair be carried out from the kitchen onto the porch. She had insisted on being put up into the highchair. She was ecstatic to be locked in behind the tray.

Her hands tapped and stroked the tray. She was not up there to eat. It was past time for that.

Behind the handsomest man on the porch was the array of green leafy trees and lawn, lit by a yard light, veiled by the black porch screen. The handsomest man smiled. He was serene.

Across from him, his wife, on the chintz flowered sofa, who was the most beautiful woman, smiled serenely at her husband. She said of her husband to the others, "He never wants to leave here. Look at him! He likes it. The food is so good and healthy. He can keep swimming in your pool. Look at him. He is so happy!"

Then the man lifted up his girl, who was smaller than the other girl, who had never ever—his girl—been irritable even once, there at that house, and he put her up onto his shoulders. Her short legs were pressing on his chest, because he had wanted her legs to do that.

Her father felt his daughter on the back of him and on the front of him, on top of him, all at once. She was slightly over his head too, her head was. Her light heels were tapping lightly on his chest. He took her hands in his. She was ready for the dive that would not be possible unless he would fling her from him.

He should.

TO DIE

I undressed myself. I wanted sex—I wanted sex—I
wanted sex—I wanted sex.
 I climbed into bed with my wife.
 She wanted sex with me. She always wants sex
with me.
 When I discharged myself this time into her, I was
feeling myself banging as high up into her as I have ever
gotten myself up into her.
 I had just done the same with another woman who
always wants sex with me, too.

There is another woman that I do the same with.

There is another woman.

There is another woman. There are five women who always want sex with me. They are always ready. It does not matter when or what or where, but they are ready.

I have a great deal of money which I have earned. I have physical beauty for a man. I have intelligence. I have work to do which I love to do, but women are what I prefer to anything, to lie down with them, the turning to touch the woman and knowing I will be received for sex as soon as I wish to be welcome.

I have been at it like this, this way for years. It does not matter when I will die. I have had everything I have ever wanted.

I should die now.

There should be a killing at my house.

There should be much, so much more for me, which I am not able to conceive of.

A CONTRIBUTION
TO THE
THEORY OF SEX

D anny Ketchem had found himself compelled, or rather, *repelled* by his lack of understanding of what had become her whole life.

It is immaterial who *she* is. She could be his wife, his mother, his daughter, his best woman friend, these, or any combination of these, or add in any other female you can think of that she could be.

What the female's life had become is also immaterial, because Danny, in any event, was bound to get confused.

Her name is Nancy Drew. Real people do have her name.

Then Danny was towering, when Nancy held him, which was her idea, and his penis was sticking itself in between her breasts, as if a button were being pushed.

Remember, Danny could be a small-sized boy standing on a stool, getting hugged by Nancy, or a tall grown-up, not on a stool, and Nancy could be short.

Some time later, but not much later, Danny was on Nancy's lap. This could happen in all of the conceivable cases.

The object—Nancy's idea—was for her to wipe that grimace off his face.

Nancy cannot, she will not bear an ugly face. She tries not to—poor schmuck. She'll try anything. I know Nancy.

I want to wipe that grin off her face. It's so easy when you're one of us.

MARRIAGE
AND THE
FAMILY

E very time I go in there I am thinking, This time
I will get the sisters straight, which one is
which. But each time I go in there I think there
is a new sister, one I have never seen before, who gets
me mixed up. This new sister will act as though she
knows me very well, as though I am quite familiar
to her.

What is the same or almost the same about all of the
sisters is this: their hair and their clothing, their faces,
their jewelry, their ages, their expressions, their atti-

tudes. I do not think they are quintuplets, if there are that many of them, or anything like that, but there is the possibility.

The sisters run a business where there are balloons around. It is a print and office supply shop in my town. It is new, and they behave as though they will be very successful, or as though they already are.

Everything is clean, such as stacks of tangerine and fuchsia paper for writing, and pens to match, which must be too expensive to buy. I wouldn't buy the pens.

Two or three of the sisters may be married. They wear tiny rectangular or round diamonds set into gold bands, and plain gold wedding bands to go with. A couple of the sisters only wear the diamonds.

There is a blond child I saw once, who looks happy and well adjusted. One of the sisters laughed and joked with the child. She hugged him and she kissed him.

A mother of a sister called in once, and she was spoken to sweetly by one of the sisters.

They do wear very tight pants. The pants hug and squeeze their bottoms so that there must be some discomfort for the sisters when they have to sit down to do their work, or even when they just stand—the pants are that tight.

I have never had an argument with one of the sisters. One of these sisters has never ridiculed me, or made me feel unwelcome, as though I were trying to take over in there, or take advantage of any of them, when I shopped there.

Not one of the sisters ever yelled at me, told me to get out of her way, or implied that I came into the shop too often, and that something was suspicious.

I never yelled back at one of the sisters to say I buy a

lot in her shop, and that I could just go somewhere else. I never said I have my whole life in my hands when I come in there. I never got myself into a rage. I never looked at a sister and thought, You frighten me more than anyone I could ever look at—take a look at you—and your whole attitude is wrong.

Your attitude is abysmal. Your attitude is as if you have been stung, or are stinging, or are getting ready to be bitten, or to bite.

The last time I was in the shop, this is what happened: a man was in there. I didn't know for what purpose. He looked suspicious. He didn't buy anything. He was darting around, and he was looking at me, and looking at me, until I had to pay attention to him. Then he said, "I saw you out there," meaning out in front of the shop. What he meant was, he had seen the way I had parked my car. I knew that had to be it. I had even surprised myself with the way I had done it. I had never done anything like that parking.

I was proud of myself like a hero should be proud, who risks his life, or who doesn't risk his life, but who saves somebody, *anybody!*

"You could have killed somebody!" was what that man said to me.

OH, MY GOD,
THE RAPTURE!

The man was looking at the woman's breasts.

The woman thought, Oh, my God, I've forgotten myself, as she saw the man, another patient, at the end of the hall, looking at her, as she realized her paper robe was open, that she had left her paper robe open like that, while she was going as she had been directed to go into another room for the cardiogram. But since he had already seen her, there was no point, she thought, to closing the robe up.

"Go in there," the nurse had said. "That's right."

Lying down, waiting for the nurse, the woman looked at the tall window that rose at her feet which to her showed a very boring sight—some greenery and sky—and then the woman thought it would be so right to have a man who was not her husband make love to her. She thought it would be the rightest thing imaginable, and she was feeling what was to her the glow of perfect good health.

It was like hand lotion, the woman thought, that the nurse was putting on her breasts in small dabs. The woman didn't look—like white—she didn't look, lotion, and it was gooey and cool, not painful, very relaxing, the whole business.

"Now don't be alarmed," the woman told the nurse, "because my cardiogram is like the cardiogram of a sixty-year-old man who has just had an attack. Did the doctor tell you not to be alarmed?"

"No," the nurse said, "not for you he didn't."

"I'm just too small in there for my heart," the woman said. "It's being squeezed, so it looks funny, and it sounds funny, but I'm all right. It's all right."

There were short black wires that the woman thought the nurse was either untangling or rearranging in the air, and to her the nurse looked happy.

The woman wanted to make the nurse even happier by chatting with her, by making the nurse laugh. But the woman's mind came to a stop on it, on the thought of it, on the thought of wanting to make someone happy.

"Oh, my God," the woman said.

The nurse opened her mouth and smiled as if she might be going to say something. She was operating the machine behind the woman's head which the woman thought was making a small unimportant noise. The whole business was so soothing, the whole cardiogram part. It was the easiest, the most relaxing thing, the woman thought.

When the doctor hung the woman's X rays up in front of her, the woman didn't even want to look.

When the doctor said, "You see, I think it's pancaked," when the doctor said, "I think it's because of your funnel chest," the woman said nothing.

"You know," the doctor said to the woman when the woman was leaving, "you ought to come in here more often."

The woman didn't have to pay the bill just then. The nurse said she did not have to, that it was not necessary, but the woman wanted to do it for the nurse.

So the woman said to the nurse, "I want to pay you now. This was wonderful. This never happens. You hardly kept me waiting at all. You took me—" she said, "you took me just when you said you would."

THE FUTURE
OF THE ILLUSION

It was an intimate relation that we had had because hardly anyone else was listening in, except for a new employee who was learning the ropes.

The clerk looked at these beans, and she said, "Those are the ones I always use." And I said, "You do?"

Then she said, "Why don't you use the canned?"

That is the finale for that. That is the end of my retelling of it, because that is the end of what I view as the significant event. Everything else about the event withers away for the retelling except for the sight of the clerk's mouth.

Questions and answers: How did the clerk and I know when enough talking was enough? I don't know. Did we care that we were deadly serious? I was surprised by it.

The clerk's upper lip is neatly scalloped. Together, her lips pout. They are the same to me as my childhood best friend's lips—the friend I had physical relations with, with a blanket over our laps on the sofa in my house.

We were girls side by side touching each other up in there where the form of the flesh is complicated. I do not know if I touched as well as she was touching me. We were about nine or we were ten, or we were eleven, or thirteen. I have no memory of sexual sensation, nor much of anything else.

I see us from the front because I am the person watching us, standing in front. I am the person who was not there at that time, who does not know whose idea it was to try, who does not know if she was the one who was afraid of being caught, if what she was doing was being done wrong.

I am still the odd man out, going backward for my training, for a feeling.

The odd woman, actually.

BOYS!

It was as if I heard a hiss come out of my mother, or she was letting me have it some way with air when I said to her *You look so beautiful.*

But she didn't do that.

What she did do was she looked at me.

Maybe not even that, because I was standing—my mouth was at her ear—when I said *You look so beautiful,* so that no one else sitting at the table would hear. Was I whispering because her face had looked to me manhandled, if that were possible, with dips and curves lying pleasingly on her, pleasingly to me on her face?

So what happened then? Because it was *her* turn. Was I pulled away to say something to someone else?

No, I think I sat back down next to her. There was no getting away from her. I had been put there with her for the meal.

But I did not look at her. I was looking to see the shine on my plate rim, the sauce shine on my meal, and I was seeing the beauty of the man next to me, which was so careful in his hair, in his wife's hair that matched his hair, in his wife's pink mouth when she spoke. And with all this beauty going on, my knife, I kept it slicing competently through my meal. I kept it slicing, and I kept putting my knife back into the correct station on the rim of my plate after having sliced.

So when my meal was finished, and I felt that it was finished with no trouble, I got up and I left the people at the table. It must have been just for a moment when I got up, which was to go to the commotion why I finally got up, not to leave my mother—because I am a mother, too, and the commotion was my problem, my children, a disorganization.

My children were going around and around the table. I think that they were going so fast that I could not have caught the sleeve of even the youngest, even if I had tried reaching out for it. I think, maybe, I did try reaching out for it. But perhaps I didn't.

They all must have been waiting for me for what I would do, everyone else at the table—all the grown-up people—but I was just looking at my children, my children going on and on, and their noise was like huge spills to me that kept being sudden and kept pouring.

And it was pleasing to me, *then it was*, in a certain way, the motion and the commotion, the children getting away from me, and I was watching it, and it was all my fault until the time when it would be over, and it wasn't as if anything could be ruined, I didn't think.

Then I called *Boys!* which I thought was loud, but when I hardly heard the word, because it was as if I had sent the word away, when the children hardly heard the word—they must not have—then I knew it must have been very faint out of my mouth, or just loud enough to be just another push of air to send them around again, to keep them going.

Then I saw a little girl, little enough that I must have missed her when she was going around with the boys, someone else's little girl, shorter than my littlest boy, that I did not know.

She must have thought she was so cute. The girl looked full of glee to me, and I was standing there, waiting for some other mother, the mother of the girl I did not know, to stand up and *do* something—because it was clear to me then that this little girl was the cause, that it was *all her fault*, and that she was the one in charge.

THE USES
OF PLEASURE

S o that's why there is no simultaneous orgasm or
hardly any or so rarely—when I can be detached, I can laugh about all those times when
you want somebody and then they don't want you and
then vice versa. Just like my aunt was saying before
they lowered my father's coffin into the grave, she
wanted to share—"Those gravediggers! If I could be
detached, this is so interesting, you know?" She was
right. They were having such a hard time steering his
coffin on the runners, or on the tracks at the turn, or on

whatever those were. They were ashamed of themselves, I could see, before they had any success. Some man who was in charge of both of them, who was even more ashamed of them than they were of themselves, had to help.

When they got my dad down finally, I turned around and saw my friend standing in back of a lot of people. She said she would come for this. I was so glad to see her. She saw me. I was so glad to see her. She seemed to me to be glad. We were both glad at the same time.

ULTIMATE
OBJECT

S he did not know there would be a cupboard full
of vases, but she had had a hunch, as when her
tongue on someone's skin could give her a hunch
of what would happen. Let me repeat—a tongue on
someone's skin.

She was with a friend with whom she could share her
joy that there was a cupboard full. She said, "We're
OK! They've got everything we could ask for!"

She was crouched, flat-footed, her body nearly into a
ball, except for her neck and for her head not conform-

ing, so that she could look into the cupboard to let all the joy which was packed inside of the cupboard for her, into her.

One plastic vase with a bulb shape, with a narrow tube protruding from the bulb upward, was light as a feather, and was as warm as plastic is.

One glass vase, the shape of a torso, was covered all over with rough-grained glass, when she took it out.

She did not let her friend take vases away when she held up vases to prove they were unsuitable because she pronounced it was so.

Each time she went down, to look in, the quality of the joy was as good, did as much for her—four times.

It was festivity.

And to her, it was festivity, the cooking or the heating, that the man who had nothing to do with either her or her friend was doing nearby at the stove.

His peaceable plan—to lift and to unfurl, flat, round, yellow, black-speckled cakes—was the only other romantic transformation—not the product of imagination—going on in the place at the same time. And the man had no more right to be in this place—he was on the same shaky ground as she was, and as her friend was, by being there—which she saw him confirm with a smile.

It did not occur to her to get close to the man, to make an advance to taste, to do anything at all consequential vis-à-vis the man.

At the risk of startling readers, there was a dead body hidden not far from the man, which was the body of a woman the man had killed the day before, with a sharp enough knife, then lying—the knife was—in a drawer above the cupboard of vases.

97

The woman's naked, somewhat hacked body, decapitated and frozen, was in the institutional-sized freezer, adjacent to the stove. Out of her swollen face, her tongue protruded.

The wrong door, for all time, had been opened.

AGAIN

Earlier, when my son was with me against his will, only for a moment, there had been a lot of baying we had heard on the radio. I had called to him, "Come hear the cattle!" but then thought, What a lie! when my son walked back out. Those had not been cattle.

On the radio—on the same program—I heard this woman saying she was better off. I was all by myself then.

She said the animals she ate were better off too. She said, "They're better off and so am I."

She said, "Most people think only of the chops and the steaks. They don't think about the ribs and the flanks and the neck."

She said, "I'll show you." She had some man there asking her questions. She said to him, "Let me show you." Then she was doing all this breathing, this gasping. She said, "God, I hate this. This happens to me every time." Then she said, "Come here, honey. Come here."

She was trying to get a lamb to come to her, I think. It was small, I imagined, like a baby lamb. She said, "Honey." She had to say it again. There was lots of wrestling that I heard.

She was wrestling with an animal which had ivory curls all over it, and gray, red-rimmed eyes, in my mind. She grabbed that baby lamb finally around the neck, her head on top of its head, I was thinking. She was hugging the baby, her pistol pressed into it somewhere, while the baby twisted to get loose, and she said, "Honey," again, and then there was this dull bang that I have heard, and the sound of falling down that I have heard.

It was at breakfast time when I heard the falling down, when I was caught next to the table I had set up for the breakfast. It was time for me to do what I do. I call.

LIFEGUARD

We had tried we had tried my mother and I to get someone to help us stop the flood in the house. We had tried to get some man. So that when my father and the man who guards my father returned, but when they were not yet inside the house, I went out to them.

That man who guards my father was sizing me up like he was wild. His head was on its side in midair bouncing, his shoulder all dipped down because I was forcing him to leave me alone with my father, and I was forcing him to go into the house to deal with the flood and with my mother, so that I was the one left guarding my father, who was wearing those shoes, who was taking those small steps toward the house. I was saying to my father, "It's not so bad, the flood. You'll see," and I was talking as slowly as he was walking in those shoes.

Those shoes on my father were the worst things I saw when I was getting him into the house, not getting him into the house, guarding him while he inched his way toward it.

Those shoes did not look like shoes that could hold a foot. There did not look to be room for a foot of flesh inside them, just a foot of bone, long like a pipe and they were forcing their way to the door of his house which was open, but from which we could not hear yet the rushing of water that I had felt rushing inside of the pipe—the hot rushing that I had seen blur the floor so that the floor was no longer a clear thing to see, so that the ceiling of our house was shedding through its lights the way rain comes down out from under a bright sun.

So that of course we were wet, my mother and I, with water binding like bracelets on our wrists, up and down our arms, like extra hair on our foreheads, on our clothes extra shapes, in our shoes which made my feet feel larger and heavier than they had ever felt.

At the door with my father, it was as if everything was hotter and wetter and louder in the house than I had remembered and was getting more so, just with us about ready to enter, and that my mother and the man who guards my father must have been the cause. They had had so much time, I thought they had, and to-gether they had not stopped it.

And then, before we ever entered, my father was telling me everything that we should do, even though I could not make it out, not the words, but I knew he was telling me how to stop the flood, if we wanted to.

THE NUB

The cantor was slumped in the winged chair on the platform behind the pulpit. For the time being, she was finished with her part.

I felt sorry for her, that we could not have given her applause for the job she had done. Something was definitely wrong when she was done, and we could not give her any applause, because she had sung her heart out.

That's what was wrong. I was thinking about the

rabbi too. How could he know it right away that I thought he was boyish and candid, so adorable and appropriate for everything he had said to the thirteen-year-old girl on this great occasion?

He had stood with the girl in front of the open ark with his hands on her. I have never seen this. He was staring into her eyes. She was staring into his eyes for how long? for how long?

A matron with a navy velvet hat on, cocked saucily, began to weep when it was her turn at the pulpit, when she said the girl's name.

Then all of that was behind us.

Then to kick off the snowball dance at the luncheon party afterward, thirteen-year-old girls asked grown men, most of whom they did not know, to dance with them, on the order of the bandleader. Dessert—a sugary baked apple with cream—was served ahead of the main course, and then there was another dessert.

I was saying all of the appropriate things to everyone to get happiness from the happiness, to have a good time at the good time and I was getting it done.

Then, with the band, the thirteen-year-old girl was singing "I'll cry if I want to," and the bandleader told her she had done a good job when she was done, and we all gave her a lot of applause.

Later, at home, on the telephone, talking to my husband, only about this and about that, when I was in the same room with my children, I was pressing the nub of myself for the pleasure of the pleasure of it—my—what I am calling the nub—call it what you like—it was at exactly the point of the corner of my bureau top. I was pressing on this nub to get aware of the possibility of the pleasure, up and down. Then I did these very gentle moves over to the side of my nub on it, while I was talking.

What I was doing to myself, just so, was working for me, but nobody could appreciate what it meant to me, except for me.

A child learns from this. Children can learn all by themselves, if they have to, not to show off.

THE WAITER

When the man turned so she could see his three-quarter profile, he was a woman for sure. So she thought, I cannot tell a man from a woman. I have to look so hard.

Then a waiter went by and she wanted to say to him, I saw you driving on the highway. I thought and thought, Who is that happy man? *Who is it?* and I thought so hard I figured it out. It was you in that dilapidated car on the highway, smiling, going north. You were going to work.

He was odd at work, the waiter, according to her, very odd and disgruntled, according to her experience with him, somewhere off. She was hoping he would not be her waiter today and lucky for her today he was not.

But he came up to her table anyway, even though he was not her waiter. From belly up was what she was seeing of him, in his red polo shirt, his yellow curls, the boy face on him, and there he was standing, and she had to wait and think so hard, Now what will he say?

According to her he was thinking hard too, so she had to wait, and then he said, "How are you today?" And then he had to wait for what she would say, his whole body from belly up not moving, waiting, until she said, "Fine."

Am I just here, she was thinking, just to make him happy? Because from belly up he sagged, she believed, as he walked away, and according to her, it was none of his business anyway how she was. Her waitress had been asking. The manager had been asking too.

Oh, she thought she was getting a revelation. Maybe he likes me. Maybe he thinks I'm pretty. Maybe he wants to know me better. Maybe he wants something more from me than "Fine" which I have just been giving away, but he does not know how to get it. He is stumped. But he is very much like a girl, isn't he. He's got one of those bow mouths. He's got those long blond lashes. He's got those curls, and there's a softness, a certain softness.

Then she saw him as though he had gotten up his momentum from just behind her table. She did not follow him apparently with her eyes to the end, to the place he was headed for, so that she did not see him pause to ask a question. She did not see him bring a thing or take it away. She did not see him disappear through any door, pass behind a wall, or turn a corner. She saw the whole length of him up and down, up and down, the white bow of his apron flapping sassy, flipping white squirts of itself up and out, to the sides, splashing, as if it were whacking itself off—the bow—according to her, all over everything.

MYSTERY OF
THE UNIVERSE

The five-year-old sitting at the head of the table said, "*Think!* You're not thinking. *Think!*"

So I tried to think, because he had said I had to.

"It has something to do with the angel," he said.

We all looked up at the lit-up Christmas tree, to the top, where I saw it pressed into the wooden beam, something golden and bent. The question, the child's question, was "What made the roof cave in?"

"He changes the rules when you start to guess it," his ten-year-old brother said.

It was true. I remembered his first hint—"It has something to do with the train," which was on tracks at the base of the tree.

The size of the child's forehead, of his whole head, is astonishing for anyone of that age, for a child of any age, for any person—the breadth and the depth and the length of it—and then at dinner it was full of the question.

"*You're not thinking!*" he said again. "*Think!*" when I said that the top of the tree had pushed through the ceiling, had made the ceiling cave in, and I am forty-two.

"No!" he said. "*That's not it!* Who can guess it what it is?"

There were two families together, guessing while we were eating. He wasn't my child with this question, but I wished that he were. He is a child to be proud of, who would force us to think, who would not let up. I didn't mind that he'd stoop to being sneaky. I was proud of him. I am proud of anyone who stands up to everyone, who would say it to everyone in front of everyone— "*You're the kind of person who would pull out a tree out of our front yard and throw it down on the house!*" I was so proud of a person who would think of doing the scariest thing he could think of, and he isn't even Jewish.

EGG

She had never allowed any egg of hers to get into such a condition, looking unlike itself and bulging, which was why the egg had all her attention from where it was in the depth of the sink, and from the depth of where it had been all dark yellow in the bowl, which had not been very far down inside the bowl, for there was no depth of anything inside the bowl, no particular depths of anything in either of her kitchen sinks either.

When she walked off from the sinks, thinking of the

egg—"How unlike itself!"—she heard a yell which was noise produced by standing water which was falling suddenly down deeply into the pipes below the sinks.

Variously, this yell was a choke to her, a slap, or the end of a life, so that she stopped when she heard the yell with her back to the sinks. She had the impression of a preamble.

This is the beginning of something.

She went and got another bad egg and gave it to the dog to eat out of the bowl, so that the bowl was scoured and banged about.

The dog, she thinks, gets everything, she was thinking later, walking the dog. He gets it, but pisses it and craps it away—daily—everything, and yet everyone shows the dog all of their love.

Even she loves and she loves and she loves the dog.

The dog goes along down the street and the people say to her, "What a nice dog," and "That's a nice-looking dog you've got there!" The dog takes her farther down the street than she intended to go, where then she is murdered.

The murderer loves and he loves the woman's dog for the rest of the dog's life. The dog loves the murderer in return. The love that they share is perfect. It is not a love that would stoop to being sexual.

WHAT WE WERE THERE FOR

She revealed a sweet temperament over and over again. Her companion kept showing her respect.

I interrupted the two of them once, before they stood to take their turn. "Mrs. Gackenback!" the secretary called.

So that's who she is! The thought expelled itself with such force from me that it startled me.

I had startled Mrs. Gackenback when I interrupted her and her companion. I interrupted Mrs. Gackenback to ask, "Was it the Pointer Sisters?"

Mrs. Gackenback told her companion, not me, that she was not sure if it had been the Pointer Sisters.

I had heard Mrs. Gackenback say to her companion just before I had interrupted them, "It wasn't the Andrew Sisters."

After being startled, Mrs. Gackenback appeared to me uncomfortable, perhaps upset, not ruined.

Mrs. Gackenback had to be helped to stand. She had to be helped to walk. Her companion did that for her.

When it was my turn, when the secretary called me, when the secretary examined me up close, she said, "You should have been a Balinese dancer." Then she said, "You do with your eyes what they can do with their hands."

I paid no attention to the secretary's hands. Her shoes were not white nurse's shoes. Her mint-green nylon dress had buttons up and down the front. Something momentous was being revealed to me which goes up and down over and over again. It was being revealed. I had to put my head down between my legs. There is nothing I can think of that is fair. There is nothing I can think of that is fair. There is nothing I can think of that is fair. There is nothing I can think of that is fair there enough. There is nothing I can think of that is there enough.

SCIENCE AND SIN
OR LOVE AND
UNDERSTANDING

I am not going to look it up in a book or do research. There are those of you who probably know why the small switching tail of a small animal makes me remember how I want to copy lewd people.

If the answer to the question is: Animals set an example for people, then I accept the answer. Do I have a choice?

I gave my husband no choice.

The last time I shoved something down my husband's throat was when I cheated on him. Now I say to him, "I didn't want to shove anything down your throat."

"It's because I love you," was the puny thing to say. It was puny compared to the size of the power which had made me say it to him.

The power had made me see things too. The power had turned him into the shape of a man wearing his clothes so he could leave me in the dark, standing beside his side of it, our bed. I knew I was seeing things.

He said, "I hear you."

I may or I may not cheat on him again. But the last time, I was standing up when I knew I was going to do it. I see myself on the street, deciding. I am holding onto something. Now I cannot see what it is. This is no close-up view. I am a stick figure.

I am the size of a pin.

ABOUT THE AUTHOR

Diane Williams coedits *StoryQuarterly*.